Magic Molly

The Wish Puppy

HOLLY WEBB

ILLUSTRATED BY ERICA JANE WATERS

Scholastic Children's Books
An imprint of Scholastic Ltd
Euston House, 24 Eversholt Street, London, NW1 1DB, UK
Registered office: Westfield Road, Southam, Warwickshire, CV47 0RA
SCHOLASTIC and associated logos are trademarks and/or
registered trademarks of Scholastic Inc.

First published in the UK as *Molly's Magic: The Wish Puppy* by Scholastic Ltd, 2009
This edition published by Scholastic Ltd, 2017

Text copyright © Holly Webb, 2009
Illustrations copyright © Erica Jane Waters, 2009

The rights of Holly Webb and Erica Jane Waters to be identified
as the author and illustrator of this work have been asserted by them.

ISBN 978 1407 17131 9

Printed by CPI Group (UK) Ltd, Croydon, CR0 4YY
Papers used by Scholastic Children's Books are made
from wood grown in sustainable forests.

3 5 7 9 10 8 6 4 2

www.scholastic.co.uk

www.holly-webb.com

For Alice, with love

Chapter One

The Saddest Puppy

Molly lay in the long grass, staring up at the sky. It was a deep end-of-summer September blue, and cloudless. It seemed to be a day for sunbathing, or picnics, or an outing, but Molly wasn't in the mood.

She couldn't help feeling a teensy bit sad. A week ago she had said goodbye to Sparkle, the wonderful, magical, *naughty* little black kitten who'd turned her life upside down. Sparkle had been lost, and he'd found Molly and asked her to help

1

him find his home again. That was when
Molly had discovered she could talk to
animals! She still had to pinch herself to
believe it was true.

Molly missed having a cheeky talking
kitten hiding out in her bedroom. She
really wanted to meet another magical
animal, now that she knew she had a
special gift. But no magical creatures had
turned up yet, and it was beginning to
feel like it had all been a dream.

"Moll-eeee! Moll-eeee!" Her little sister

Kitty was standing on the orchard gate, calling to her. "Molly, where are you? I need you to *play* with me!"

Molly thought about just staying where she was. The grass was long, and there was a good chance Kitty couldn't see her. She didn't much want to play mermaids, Kitty's favourite game of the moment.

Then a thought struck her. *I wonder if there really are mermaids,* she said to herself, her eyes widening. *If there are actual witches, and kittens who can talk, maybe mermaids are real too! Oh, I wish we were going to the seaside soon!* Her nana lived by the sea, and Molly could imagine walking along the beach and finding a mermaid hiding in a rockpool, her hair like swirling seaweed.

Molly stood up, her head full of mermaids and sparkling sea, but Kitty had already run off to find someone else to join in her game.

"Molly!" It was her dad now, calling her from the vet's surgery on the other side of the old farmyard. He was looking out of the window at her. "Molly, do you want to come over? It's nearly the end of morning surgery, I could do with a helper. Mrs Hunter's brought her new puppy to see me. I'm sure she'd love to show her off."

"What sort of dog is she?" Molly asked excitedly.

"She's a spaniel, a King Charles spaniel. Lovely dogs. Mrs Hunter needs some company, and small dogs like those don't need too much walking. She's just bringing

Star in because she's a new puppy. It's always good to get a new pet checked over."

Molly ran across the yard and pushed open the door to the surgery, bumping into Jenny, the veterinary nurse, as she was coming out.

"Hi Molly! Are you coming to visit your dad?"

Molly nodded. "He said I could see Mrs Hunter's new puppy," she told Jenny excitedly.

Jenny smiled. "The puppy looked quite shy – I think she needs your 'magic touch', Molly!"

Molly nodded happily and went in to the consulting room. "Hi Dad! Hi, Mrs Hunter!"

Mrs Hunter was an elderly lady that Molly had known for ages from her visits to the surgery. Molly had been really sad when Mrs Hunter's last dog, a Westie called Morris, had died earlier in the year. But her dad had pointed out that Morris was fourteen, which was a good age for a dog. Mrs Hunter had missed him loads, though, and it had taken her a while to decide she wanted another dog.

"Ohhh, she's gorgeous!" Molly breathed, as she caught sight of the little golden brown

 and white dog. The puppy was peeping out over Mrs Hunter's arm, looking nervously round the surgery.

Mrs Hunter smiled, but she didn't look quite as happy as Molly

thought someone with a beautiful new puppy should.

Molly's dad patted Star as Mrs Hunter put her on the examining table. The puppy was mostly a soft golden colour, with gorgeous, long brown ears, and a few pretty chestnut spots on her back. "She's beautiful! She came from somewhere round here, did you say?"

Mrs Hunter nodded. "Yes, I got her from a farm not far away. They breed dogs too, they have a lovely kennels in one of their barns." She stroked the little dog's head gently, but the look she gave her was anxious.

"And how's she settling in?" Molly's dad tickled the puppy under the chin, but she was crouched on the table looking scared.

Molly looked at her worriedly. There was something odd here. A lot of dogs

were scared to be at the vet's – her dad
was always very careful about which
animals Molly was allowed to touch, in
case a frightened creature bit her – but
this seemed different. Star looked so sad!

Mrs Hunter smiled. "Well – it's

different. I suppose I'm still missing
Morris a little. But Star is lovely. I'm sure
we'll soon settle down together."

Molly's dad nodded. "It just takes time.

She looks very loving." He went over to the shelves to get the equipment for Star's vaccinations, and the little dog watched him quietly. She didn't even flinch though, just hung her head, her whiskers brushing the table.

"Can I stroke her?" Molly asked, desperate to cheer the puppy up, and Mrs Hunter nodded. Molly gently ran her hand down Star's back, admiring her silky fur. But then she stood back, blinking. She could *feel* Star's sadness. The puppy was so unhappy! This wasn't just a young dog taking a while to settle in, something was wrong.

Very carefully, Molly lifted Star up and cuddled her. Most puppies would have wriggled and squirmed in excitement, but Star just lay limply in Molly's arms. Molly stroked her gently, and a wave of loneliness washed over her, a feeling that she'd lost someone very special. The sadness was so strong that Molly felt like crying and she almost dropped Star in surprise.

Star suddenly gave a little squeak and lifted her head, her huge brown eyes sparkling with hope. She put a paw on Molly's arm and gazed up at her. Molly's mind was suddenly filled with a joyful whisper.

"You can hear me!"

Chapter Two

Star's Story

Star wasn't ill, so after she'd had her vaccinations, Mrs Hunter picked her up to take her home. Molly really wanted to say something, to stop her, but how could she? Mrs Hunter and Dad wouldn't understand if she told them something was wrong. Star looked perfectly healthy.

Star had scrabbled a little as Mrs Hunter carried her out of the surgery, gazing over her owner's shoulder at Molly. Her eyes were pleading, and Molly was sure she could hear her still. *Please, please help me. . .*

Star kept popping into Molly's head all week. Especially those big, dark-brown puppy eyes. She had found another magical animal! Molly wanted to dance, she was so excited, but at the same time  she couldn't help worrying what was wrong with Star. Molly was sure that she'd never *felt* anything so strong from a dog before. It was just like the magical energy that had rushed through her when she had first touched Sparkle, the kitten.

Molly had always been good at

understanding what animals wanted, but this had been different. Molly just wished she'd said something back, told Star she had understood.

I shouldn't have let her go! Molly thought to herself crossly. *Why did I? It was just such a shock, I didn't think. I really have to find Star, and help her. She asked me to!*

But Molly didn't even know where Mrs Hunter lived, or she'd have tried to get Mum to go that way for some reason. Larkfield wasn't a big town, she was sure she could have made something up! Now all she could do was look out for Mrs Hunter and Star while she was on her way to school, or out with Mum and Kitty.

As they were coming home from school on Wednesday, Molly spotted a lady in the High Street with a dog that looked

just like Star. Funnily enough, it wasn't
the dog's golden brown fur that made
her so sure it was Star. Instead it was the
sad way the dog's ears were drooping.
Mrs Hunter was looking down at her
worriedly as the little dog trailed along at
the end of her pretty red lead.

Without even thinking, Molly chased
after them. She was halfway down the
street before Mum noticed she was gone,
and called after her in horror. "Molly!
Come back!"

Molly hesitated. She knew she had to go back, or Mum would be really cross, but it was Star! Just there! And she still looked so sad, and in need of Molly's help. Molly gave Mum an apologetic look and turned to keep running.

But it was too late. Mrs Hunter was already disappearing round the corner. Just as Star turned the corner of the street, she looked back, and Molly thought she saw a sudden flash of hope in the puppy's big dark eyes. But then she was gone, into the crowd.

Molly sighed, and walked slowly back to Mum and Kitty. Mum was furious with her for running off, and she hadn't even been able to help!

Then at lunch on Saturday, Molly's dad said, between bites of ham sandwich, that Star was back. Molly hadn't been able to

visit the surgery that morning — Mum
had taken her and Kitty clothes shopping
because it was turning cold and Molly
had grown a lot over the summer.

Molly choked on her juice. "What do
you mean, she's back?" she spluttered. "Is
she all right?"

Her dad frowned. "I honestly don't
know, Molly. Mrs Hunter said that Star's
stopped eating, which is very worrying.
I'm keeping Star here for the moment to
do some tests and try to work out what's
wrong."

"Can I come and see her?" Molly
asked eagerly.

Her dad nodded. "Maybe you can cheer
her up a bit."

Molly smiled gratefully at him. She just
hoped that when she saw Star she'd be
able to talk to her properly this time.

After lunch Molly and her dad walked back across the yard to the surgery.

"Do you think Star might be really sick, Dad?" Molly asked quietly. She knew that sometimes her dad just couldn't help. Everyone at the surgery hated it when that happened.

Molly's dad shook his head. "I don't think so, at the moment. I can't see anything wrong with her."

"Can I go and keep her company?" Molly's voice was hopeful.

"Yes, I've got quite a few cases coming

in this afternoon. Just be gentle, won't you? She's such a shy little dog." Her dad grinned and put an arm round her as they opened the surgery door. "I don't need to tell you that, do I, Molly? Probably you'll have Star all sorted out by the time I get through my appointments."

Molly smiled back. Of course her dad was joking, but she was so hoping that actually he was right. . .

Molly quietly opened the door to the animal ward. It was empty apart from the large run at the end, where Star was curled up on a comfy cushion. She was facing the wall, and she didn't even bother to turn round when Molly came in. Molly opened the run, and knelt by the door.

"Hey, Star," she murmured, trying not to scare the little dog.

Star peered over her shoulder wearily, and politely sniffed Molly's fingers.

Molly shivered. She had to find out what was wrong. She reached into the cage and lifted the puppy out. At last Star looked up, and a mist seemed to clear away from her eyes.

"It's you!" she breathed. "I remember you!" She jumped up and stood with her front paws on Molly's chest, looking into her face. "You're magical too, I could feel it. You wanted to help me!"

Molly nodded slowly. The worry about Star was seeping away from her mind now, and she could feel the excitement bubbling up inside her. Star was talking to her!

Molly shook herself. That wasn't what was important right now. "What's wrong, Star? Have you lost your owner? Or is it that you don't like Mrs Hunter? She's really nice, you know."

"No, no!" Star shook her head so that her long ears flapped prettily. "She's lovely. She misses her old dog, I can tell, but I know I'll be happy there. I could make her happy too, I know we could, if only. . ." She sighed, and looked miserably at Molly.

"She only took me," Star whispered, and Molly could feel that it hurt her to talk about it. "We tried to tell her, Stella and I, but she couldn't hear us. We *have* to be together. We're twins, but it's more than that. We're wish puppies. We belong together – when Stella and I are together, we can do anything," she added proudly. "We can grant you any wish you like!"

Molly laughed delightedly. "I knew it! I knew there was something special about you. Magic twin puppies, that's so amazing! Can you really grant wishes? If I wished for something now, would it really come true?"

Star looked thoughtfully at Molly, with her head on one side and her lip curling a little in a shy dog smile. "What is your absolute favourite thing to eat?" she asked.

"What would you like best right this minute?"

Molly licked her lips just thinking about it. "Mint choc-chip ice cream! With chocolate sauce, like my mum makes sometimes."

Star hopped off Molly's knee and sat in front of her in a perfect china dog pose. She closed her eyes, and went very still.

There was a sudden shimmer of purple sparkles all around them and a pretty pink bowl dropped into Molly's hands. Molly gasped excitedly and then gulped.

It wasn't ice cream. The bowl was full of broccoli, Molly's worst ever food, that she was always arguing with Mum over. Molly was disappointed for a second, but then the funny side of it struck her. Magic broccoli! She giggled.

Star was gazing anxiously into the bowl. "That isn't right, is it?" she asked slowly.

"No. . . But it's a beautiful bowl," Molly added quickly, not wanting to upset her.

Star's ears drooped. "I should have been able to do that," she murmured worriedly. "I knew it. I could feel it. It's fading. I'm losing my magic, Molly!"

"What do you mean?" Molly asked in horror. She picked Star up and cuddled her close, feeling the little dog's heart banging against her ribs.

"It's because I'm not with Stella," Star muttered miserably into Molly's jumper. "We usually do magic together, but a little thing like a bowl of ice cream, I shouldn't need Stella for that. The magic is going. Maybe it's gone already!" Her voice was shaking.

"No, no, it can't be," Molly told her, hoping she was right. "If it had gone, nothing would have happened when you tried to make the ice cream. I know the magic didn't work the way it was supposed to, but even broccoli coming out of nowhere is pretty special, you know."

"Perhaps," Star murmured. "But what

can I do? The longer Stella and I are apart, the weaker we'll get. Oh, Molly, I have to find her!"

"*We* have to find her," Molly said firmly. "I'll help." She thought back to Star's first visit to the surgery. "Mrs Hunter said she got you from a farm not far from here. Do you know where it is?"

Star shook her head, but already she was looking more hopeful. Molly guessed that Star really needed another person to talk to – she just wasn't used to being without Stella. "I was in a box, and I was crying for Stella, so I wasn't really thinking. But you're right, it can't have been far. Oh, Molly, now you're here, I know we can find her! I knew you were special from the first time you picked me up!"

Molly smiled at her, and stroked her fluffy ears. "I'm sure we can too. There are lots of farms round here, but I shouldn't think many of them breed dogs. We should be able to work out which one it is, no problem." *But then what are we going to do?* Molly suddenly wondered. *I can't kidnap a puppy!*

Chapter Three

A Midnight Trip

"How's it going, Molly?" Molly's dad put his head round the door, and Molly tried not to look guilty. She hadn't actually been doing anything wrong, but she didn't fancy explaining that Star could talk. She scooted the bowl of broccoli behind her with her foot.

"I think Star's just lonely," Molly told her dad.

"She definitely looks a bit happier

now." Molly's dad crouched down to look. "I need to have a proper look at her, and your mum says to tell you to go back and do your homework, OK?"

Molly sighed. "OK." She gave Star one last hug, and whispered in her ear, "Don't worry, I'll be back, I promise."

Star rubbed her silky ears against Molly's cheek, and then let Molly pass her over to her dad. As Molly's dad carried her back into the consulting room, Star was staring over his shoulder at Molly

all the way. Molly could hear her secret message, and see it in her eyes.

Come back soon. We need you, Molly. We're running out of time!

Molly threw the broccoli away in the kitchen bin. Then she carried the pink bowl up to her room to admire while she was doing her reading for school. She couldn't concentrate though. All she could think of was how to find Stella, and bring her and Star back together.

Maybe she could look up dog-breeders on the computer? Then she had a brilli idea. Dad's map! He had on with all the farms in the are got called out to see a sic nipped quickly down an from the drawer in the

Back in her room,

on the bed. Wow, there were lots! But Molly knew some of the closer ones. None of them had dogs. And that one, Sweethill Farm, wasn't that where Sam from school lived? Sam's parents only had chickens. It took ages but at last Molly had a list of six farms – one of them had to be Star's old home. Molly went back to her homework, glancing

occasionally at the list, as though it might tell her something. She couldn't wait to show it to Star.

"Molly, will you come and play with me? You haven't played with me all day!" Kitty pleaded, running in and bouncing on the end of Molly's bed.

Molly smiled at her little sister. She looked a bit like Star, with big, begging brown eyes. "All right. What do you want to play?" Molly checked her watch quickly. When was she going to fit in going back to the surgery? It was nearly tea time, almost the end of surgery hours, and Mum and Dad wouldn't let her go over there when no one else was around. Perhaps she could nip back now? She'd been doing her reading for ages – or holding the book, at least. But Kitty was happily chattering on about the game they were going to play. She couldn't tell Kitty she wasn't going to play with her now.

But when was she going to go? She couldn't wait until tomorrow. What if Star's magic was running out this very minute? Molly had to tell her the names of the farms, to see if she remembered which was hers.

Actually, it would be better to be at the surgery when no one else was there, if only she was allowed. Then there wouldn't be anyone to walk in and catch her talking to Star. As Molly walked over to the meadow with Kitty, a daring plan formed in her mind, making her smile excitedly to herself, and shiver, just a little bit. The only time she could go to the surgery in secret was at night. The *middle* of the night. She was going to have to go on a midnight mission!

"Night, Molly. Sleep well." Molly's mum gave her a hug, and Molly snuggled under her duvet, trying to look sleepy. She was sure she wouldn't be able to get to sleep, but she didn't want Mum to be suspicious.

As soon as her mum had shut the door, Molly sat up, and grabbed her pink kitten alarm clock from the bookshelf by her bed. It meowed when the alarm went off, which always made her laugh. Molly set it for midnight, and tucked it carefully under her pillow. She didn't want to wake up anyone else in the house as well. Luckily Mum and Dad both went to sleep pretty early normally. Then she lay down again and sighed. Of course she wouldn't be able to sleep, she thought, yawning. And it was only eight o'clock. Four hours until she set off! What on earth was she going to do? Molly's eyes closed and then fluttered open, and she yawned. Waiting was so boring. . .

Molly jumped awake as the muffled mewing sounded in her ear. She shook her head sleepily, trying to work out what was going on. Oh! The alarm clock! Her special mission! Somehow it didn't seem so exciting in the middle of the night, when her bedroom was so very dark. And it was cold. Molly rummaged under her pillow and turned off the alarm, then sat up. She shivered, but threw back her duvet.

It was
dark for Star
too, down in
the surgery,
and she
was waiting
for Molly.
She'd been waiting ages, and she probably
thought Molly had given up.

Molly put on her dressing gown,
tucking the list into the pocket. She'd
grab her wellies to cross the yard when
she got downstairs. She'd hunted out her
torch before she went to bed, and now
she grabbed it and set off, trying not
to feel scared. It was only her house! It
wasn't as if she was going far – just across
the yard. In the dark.

Molly crept along the landing, trying
to remember which were the creaky

steps on the stairs. The farmhouse was old, and there were often strange noises in the night. Dad always said it was just the pipes. So hopefully Mum and Dad wouldn't get up if they heard anything.

Molly made it to the kitchen and breathed a sigh of relief. No one would hear her down here. Now, the keys. Mum kept them all on hooks on the wall. Yes! Here were the surgery keys, and the back door key to let herself out.

Funnily enough, it seemed lighter outside. The moon was shining brightly as Molly set off across the yard, unlike her torch which was worryingly feeble. It must be low on batteries. Molly shook it hopefully, but it made no difference. She couldn't stop to look for batteries now, she'd just have to manage.

Molly went on, and then realized she

was crunching across the gravel. She tried
to tiptoe but her wellies wouldn't bend
that way. She froze, and stared up at her
parents' window, but the light didn't go
on. Luckily it was a bit chilly for having

the windows open. Maybe the best thing
to do was just run and get to the surgery
as quickly as she could.

Molly flung herself across the yard and
arrived, heart thudding, at the back door
that went straight into the animal ward.
She fumbled for the right key, and at last
the door clicked open.

The room looked strange in the dark,
much bigger. Molly shone the torch
around, and eyes gleamed spookily out
of the darkness. Something was watching
her! Molly gasped, and then sighed out
a breath, her heartbeat slowing down
again. It was only the cats. Her dad had
mentioned that there were a couple of
cats in the ward that night, as he'd kept
them in that afternoon. He'd grumbled,
laughing, because he was going to have to
get up early to check on them.

Both the cats mewed hopefully at her, wondering if she was bringing them some food, and Molly went up to their pens. "Sorry, I haven't got anything for you," she murmured, reaching her fingers through and gently stroking them behind the ears, making them purr faintly. "I've just come to talk to Star."

Star was standing up in her pen, waiting anxiously for Molly. She looked like a little pale ghost in the torchlight. Was it Molly's imagination, or was Star herself fading away, not only her magic? Did wish puppies disappear, when they

couldn't grant wishes? That would be awful!

Molly let Star out of the pen and they curled up together in the old armchair that the veterinary nurses used when they had to feed baby animals.

"I'm so glad you came back," Star murmured, pressing her nose gratefully into Molly's neck. "I miss Stella so much, but you being here helps."

"I've been trying to think how we could find Stella," Molly told her. "I had an idea, look. I found my dad's map with all the farms round here on it. This is a list of farms that might be your one. Do you think you'd recognize the name of it?"

Star said, "Maybe. . ." but she sounded doubtful, and when Molly told her the names on the list, her eyes misted over with that strange, sad look again. "I don't remember any of them, Molly," she whispered.

"Don't worry." Molly tried to make her voice bright, but she knew it wasn't very convincing. "I'm sure it's one of those. We'll just have to try them all, somehow. . ."

But how? Molly didn't know but she wasn't going to give up. They *had* to find Stella. She hugged Star close, feeling the glittery, wonderful sense of magic running through the fur under her fingertips. "I don't suppose you could use your magic to search for Stella?" she asked hopefully.

"I did try, when I was first taken away," Star explained. "But I was so upset then, I couldn't find anything. Maybe if I try again now."

She sat up tensely on Molly's knee,

staring into the distance, clearly thinking hard about her sister. Her eyes sparkled for a second, and Molly took a hopeful breath. Was the magic about to work?

But then the magical light died away, and Star flopped sadly down on Molly's lap. "I can't make it work at all. I can hardly feel my magic, Molly. Without Stella, it's nearly all gone." Her voice was shaking, and her tiny body shook too.

Molly ran her hand down Star's silky

back. "It'll be all right. We'll find the farm," she promised her firmly. "I'll go back home and look on the computer now. If I search for those farms, one of them might have a website about breeding spaniels. We'll find her, Star. We really will."

Chapter Four

The Wishing Spell

Molly scurried carefully across the gravel
again. She was planning to use the
computer in the study and search the
internet to see if one of those six farms
was advertising King Charles spaniel
puppies. Surely there wouldn't be more
than one? She really hoped they did have
a website, or a mention somewhere. They
did lots of research on the computers at
school, so she was pretty sure she could
find it. Oh, if only Star had been able

to use her magic even a little, just to give her some clues. But she couldn't do magic without her twin to help. She needed someone to join with. . .

Molly stopped suddenly in the middle of the yard, putting her hand up to the locket round her neck, the little cat face that Sparkle and the witch had given her. It had one of Sparkle's whiskers in it, so Molly could call him for help.  She could feel the locket glowing in her fingers as a wonderful idea came to her. Star needed someone to join with, but did it have to be Stella? Maybe she should call Sparkle now? Perhaps he could join with Star, and help her use her magic?

Molly could feel the power of the locket in her hand. She thought about that wonderful, scary afternoon, when she'd taken Sparkle home. The witch had said Molly had a true gift for helping animals. Her magic wasn't only to talk to them, she could *do* things too. Molly and Sparkle had made a magic dust together – Molly really had helped him, even though she wasn't sure how. She could do things. . .

Maybe she didn't need to call Sparkle. Maybe there was a way that Star could use Molly's own magic to help her find Stella?

Molly was so excited that she forgot about being careful. She just ran back, waving her torch wildly. And she was so eager to find Star again that she didn't realize her torch batteries had finally given up. She was bathed in a silvery light as she tried to unlock the door with trembling fingers. At last she flung it open and raced back into the surgery. The two cats hissed with surprise as she burst in, and Star jumped up at the wire of her pen.

"Molly!" she barked. "You're shining!"

Molly looked down at her hands in surprise. Star was right. There was a silvery glow all round her, gleaming softly from her skin. Wow! That had never happened before. She turned her hands over, wiggling her fingers. It was still there!

Star scrabbled eagerly at the door of

her pen. She suddenly seemed more alive than Molly had ever seen her, her tail wagging with excitement. "Let me out! Molly, quickly, please!"

Molly undid the latch. "What's happening, Star? Did you do this? Is your magic coming back after all?" she asked hopefully.

"No, this must be your power, Molly! But that light, it's just like what happens when Stella and I do magic – except our light is pink. Don't you see what that means? Maybe you and I could do magic together to find Stella!"

Molly laughed delightedly. "But that's what I was coming back to say! I thought of it just now. I remembered that the witch told me I should use my power to help. I thought I might be able to take Stella's place, just this once."

Star nodded seriously. "I'm sure we can."

"What do we have to do?" Molly demanded, her voice eager.

Star sniffed the air thoughtfully. "We should go outside. We need to call to Stella, and we can't be shut in for that. Where's a good place, Molly?" She looked up at Molly, her deep, dark eyes shining with hope and love. It was love for Stella, but for Molly too, and it made Molly feel so special, knowing that Star trusted her.

I can't let them down! she told herself fiercely. *We have to do this — Star looks so much better already, just thinking that we might find Stella. She'd almost given up before.*

"The orchard?" Molly suggested. "It's beautiful there. Would that help?"

Star nodded. "If it's a special place for you, then it will be good for doing magic. Let's go, Molly!" She was dancing and jumping round Molly's legs, looking more like a puppy than Molly had ever seen her.

The silver glow lit their way as they opened the orchard gate. Star ran ahead, bouncing through the long grass, her ears flapping wildly. The moonlight was shining on the last of the apples, the ones at the tops of the trees that were too high to reach.

Star looked round at Molly. "This is the place," she said. "Molly, will you pick me up? We should be touching for the magic to work."

Molly scooped Star up in her arms,
and together they stared into the sky.
Molly felt Star's magic shimmering into
her own, and the silver light around
them became tinged with pink. The
warm glow of the magic seemed to
run through her body, and she shivered

delightedly and buried her face in Star's silky fur.

"Ohhh, wonderful," Star murmured. "It's like I haven't been able to breathe, and now I can. Now wish, Molly! Wish for Stella to come back to us!"

Molly nodded, and she whispered to the sky, "I'm wishing! I'm wishing!"

Star made a little whining noise. "Stella, can you hear us? We're wishing for you! Please come and find us. . . I need you. . ."

Molly sighed. How would they know if it was working? Had her power helped Star to make the wish come true?

All at once a cloud of silver stars rushed into the sky,

sparkling and shimmering, and carrying
the wish with them.

Molly gasped with delight.

"That was it," Star said proudly.

"Oh! Does that mean it's worked?"
Molly asked hopefully.

Star stared up at the stars glittering
above them, the star-shine reflected in her
dark eyes. "I hope so, Molly. I've never
made a wish for myself before, but this is
the most important wish of all. I hope it
comes true. . ."

The wish stars flickered upwards until
Molly and Star couldn't tell them apart
from the real stars any more. Then the
two of them sank down on to the grass,
worn out with the effort of wishing.

They had done everything they could.
Now they just had to wait.

Chapter Five

Star and Stella

Molly shivered and hugged Star tight. "It's getting cold," she whispered. "We should go back."

Star gave a reluctant whine, looking sadly up at Molly. Her eyes still shimmered with the silver wish-light, but she looked small and lonely. Molly stared at the tiny dog in her arms. Molly couldn't leave her to sleep on her own in that little pen, even though it did have a warm cushion, and chew toys.

"I know, but we can't stay out here all night. I wish we could, but we'll freeze." Molly stroked Star's ears gently. "I won't put you back in your pen," she muttered. "You're coming back to the house with me, Star." Molly didn't know what would happen in the morning, when Mum found Star in her room. She would get into trouble, but all of a sudden she was too tired to care.

She stood up, holding Star in her arms, and trudged slowly to the gate, and across the yard. At the back door, Molly paused, and they gazed up into the sky. Was it her imagination, or were there still a few wish sparkles floating there? Was it going to work? It just had to! "*Please. . .*" Molly murmured, not quite sure who she was talking to.

They crept up the stairs, a faint silver

light still glowing around them and
lighting their way. Star looked around
interestedly as they sneaked up into
Molly's room. "This is nice," she said
sleepily, curling into a small shining ball on
Molly's duvet. Molly started to answer her,
but then realized that the puppy was fast
asleep. Obviously wishing was hard work!

Molly hung up her dressing gown, yawning hugely. Seeing Star all snuggled up like that made her feel so sleepy too. She crawled carefully under the duvet, trying not wake up Star, who'd chosen a place right in the middle of the bed. Molly ended up with her nose pressed against the wall, but she didn't mind. Star's peaceful breathing shushed in her ears, and she drifted off to sleep.

"Hey," Molly murmured sleepily. She was having a strange dream. Somebody was licking her — it felt like a dog. Whoever it was, they were very determined about it. They kept going, even when she tried to wriggle away. Eventually Molly realized that she wasn't dreaming. There really *was* a dog very thoroughly licking her ear. Star! Molly sat bolt

upright, suddenly remembering her
adventures of the night before.

"At last! I've been trying to wake you for ages!" Star was bouncing up and down on the bed beside her, her ears flapping joyfully.

Molly stared at her, slowly taking in how different she looked. Star's eyes were shining with happiness. She'd lost the strange, ghostly look that had made it look as though she was only half there. Her coat was thick and glossy, her brown patches shining as though she'd been polished. Altogether she looked like a different dog from the sad, quiet little creature of yesterday.

"Come on!" Star barked happily. "Ooops, sorry, Molly!" She stuck her head under the duvet, giggling. Then she wriggled further down, enjoying her game, and little pink sparkles trickled out from under the edges of the duvet.

It looked like Star's power was well and truly back.

Even though she was worried about Mum or Dad hearing, Molly couldn't help laughing too. Star's happiness was filling the room.

Star's black nose peeped out from under the duvet. "Come on!" she said again, whispering this time. "Stella's near, I can feel her! Come *on*, Molly!"

Molly jumped out of bed. "She's here already? Oh, Star, that's wonderful!" Molly scrambled into jeans and a jumper, and they raced downstairs. Molly hadn't bothered to look at her clock in the rush, but she was sure it was still quite early. It didn't feel like she'd had very much sleep, but she was too excited to feel tired.

Star was jumping and scrabbling eagerly

at the back door. "She's here, Molly, she's here! Let me out!"

Molly unlocked the door, and swung it open, looking anxiously out into the yard.

Sitting on the back step was a beautiful little dog, staring up at her with hopeful eyes. Molly gasped. She was the image of Star! The same gorgeous fluffy ears; big, dark eyes, and cute snub nose. Even the identical joyful expression as the two puppies flung themselves at each other with delighted little whines.

"It worked! Oh, Star, it worked!" Molly murmured, watching the two puppies rubbing their heads together lovingly. She crouched down beside them. "I can't believe how alike you look. Even the spots on your backs are the same."

Stella looked up at her. "They're not quite the same, you know," she said, her voice a softer version of Star's, as though perhaps she wasn't as used to talking to people. "Look. . ." And she and Star sat down together with their backs turned to Molly, each peering over their shoulder and giving her dog-smiles, their pink tongues showing.

"Oh! Yes, I can see now. They're opposites, aren't they? Like you're one dog looking in a mirror. It's so pretty, it's almost as though the spots join up." Molly turned her head to one side. "They do! It's a heart shape, a perfect heart!"

The dogs nodded at her. "That's why we're wish puppies, Molly," Star explained.

"We're *very* rare," Stella added.

"And now we're together, we can grant wishes again." Star touched noses joyfully with Stella.

"How did you do it, Star?" Stella asked. "I'd worn myself out wishing for you to come back, but it never worked. Without you I just couldn't make the wishes happen. I'd given up. I was sure I wouldn't ever be a magic dog again, and then last night I felt a wish sparkling all over me. It woke me up and I felt so happy. Then suddenly I was outside my run, and there was a trail of silver stars glittering in the grass. I followed them, they smelled delicious, like the best dog biscuits. And they led me here."

"It was Molly," Star said, staring up at her gratefully. "She wanted to help, but we couldn't work out how. Then I saw her glowing, like we do when we make wishes, and I thought perhaps she could be a wish-girl, to get you back for me. And it worked!"

"I've never heard of a wish-girl." Stella looked at Molly admiringly. "You know what this means, don't you, Star?" she told her twin.

Star nodded. "Definitely."

The pair of them gazed up at Molly, and she stepped back worriedly. "What is it?"

"You've saved us, Molly. You've brought us back together, so now we will give you a wish. A very special wish, to say thank you. What do you want most of all?" Star and Stella had tiny pink sparkles twinkling over their fur already, and Molly was pretty sure that whatever she wished for, she would get. No magic broccoli this time. But what should she ask for? A wish! It was so special, so important. She mustn't waste it.

All at once, Molly knew. It was what she had wanted for so long. She closed her eyes, ready to speak the words aloud—

But then she had a sudden thought. She opened her eyes again, looking down worriedly at the puppies. *What was going to happen to them now?* Mrs Hunter had only wanted one dog. Would she take Stella as well? And how was Molly going to explain that Star's twin had suddenly appeared? Dad wasn't going to believe it, whatever she said.

Molly sighed. She knew what her wish had to be. She closed her eyes again.

"I wish that Star and Stella find a home together," she said firmly. "And that they make Mrs Hunter happy." She smiled as she said that last bit. Even though it was disappointing not to use the wish for herself, she could just imagine Star and Stella dragging Mrs Hunter all over the town, and the old lady laughing.

She opened her eyes again, and sat down on the step with a bump. Star and Stella were surrounded by a beautiful pink

and purple cloud, and the heart shape
on their backs seemed to glow. Then the
colours faded, and the wish puppies shook
themselves.

"Oh, Molly!" Star said, surprised. "That was supposed to be a wish for you!"

"It was for me!" Molly smiled at her. "I'd be ever so worried about you, wouldn't I, if I hadn't done it? Besides, maybe that wish will stop Dad finding out I went into the surgery in the middle of the night!" she added. "He'd be really cross!"

"She deserves another wish, since she used her wish for us," Stella said firmly. "I could do another, Star, couldn't you? I can tell you had something else you wanted, Molly, I could see it in your eyes."

"Of course I could!" Star said indignantly. "Molly has a loving heart. We should definitely give her another wish."

The two puppies stared up at her expectantly, and Molly smiled. "I'm so glad you're going to find a home," she whispered to them. "I know you'll be happy. But my wish is that one day, I don't mind when, really, as long as it isn't too long. . . One day, please could I have a pet of my own?"

Star and Stella looked at each other and nodded.

"Oh yes!" Star breathed. "It's a good wish!"

"A special wish!" Stella agreed, and once again the pink and purple swirling mist rippled around them, and this time Molly felt silvery threads wrapping round her too. There was a wonderful floating feeling as the mist swept round her, shimmering in and out and through – and then it was gone, leaving just a sense of happiness.

"It worked, didn't it?" Molly asked, as

the puppies blinked sleepily at her.

"Oh yes. . ." Star yawned. "Sorry, Molly,

70

I'm tired. Two wishes at once is ever such a lot. We even had to borrow some of your magic again to make sure." She climbed into Molly's lap, and curled up snugly. "Come on, Stella," she murmured, and the second wish puppy followed her sister, nudging her over to make room.

"You need a bigger lap," she told Molly, as she fell asleep.

Molly smiled down at them, one ball of brown and gold fur, and she leaned

against the door frame and closed her
eyes too, dreaming of her own pet, at
last. . .

Read on for an extract from Holly
Webb's brand new series about Sophie
and her super squeaky and furry friends!

CHAPTER ONE

Sophie peered out over the view, watching the sunlight sparkle on the windows, and wondering who lived there, under the roofs. She couldn't see her own house from here, or she didn't think she could, anyway. She hadn't lived in Paris for long enough to know.

The city *was* very beautiful, but it still
didn't feel like home. Sophie sighed, and
rested her chin on her hands. She missed
her old house, and her old bedroom, and
her cat, Oscar. Grandma was looking

after him while they lived in Paris, but Sophie was sure that Oscar missed her, almost as much as she missed him.

"What are you looking at?" Dan squashed up next to her, leaning over the stone balcony.

"Just things," Sophie said vaguely. "The view."

"Boring," Dan muttered. "This is taking ages. And I'm hungry." He turned round, holding his tummy in both hands and made a starving face at Sophie. His nose scrunched up like a rabbit's, and Sophie smirked. She crossed her eyes and poked her tongue out at the corner of her mouth to make Dan laugh. After all, even a wonderful view can be boring when you've been looking at it for a *VERY LONG TIME.*

All the people who live in Paris love their city so much, and many of them walk up the steep steps to the church on their wedding days to have their photographs taken next to the wonderful view. But it can take an awful long time to get the photographs right, especially when it's windy and your auntie's wedding dress won't stay still properly.

"Sophie and Dan! Stop making faces like that! You're making Dad giggle, and he's supposed to be taking romantic photos!" Mum glared at them, but Dad rolled his eyes, and stuck his tongue out at Dan. Sophie thought Dad might be a bit bored with the photos as well.

This church was one of Sophie's favourite places in Paris. It was so pretty, and there was the fountain to look at, and all the people. She even liked its name, *Sacré Coeur*, which meant Sacred Heart. Sophie thought it was very special to have a whole church that was all about love. Auntie Lou's wedding had been beautiful too, but Sophie had got up early for Mum to curl her hair and fuss over her dress, and she was tired of having to stand still and smile.

"Go and play," Auntie Lou suggested.

"Go and run around for a bit. You can come back and be in the photos later."

"Later?" Dad moaned. "I thought we'd nearly finished!" But Sophie and Dan were already halfway down the white marble steps, and couldn't hear him.

"I wish we'd brought a ball..." Dan said, as they stopped in front of the fountain that stood below the balcony. He was looking at the grassy slope of the hill. "Do you think Mum would mind if we went home and got one? It wouldn't take five minutes."

"Yes, she would! And anyway, even *you* couldn't play football on that grass," Sophie pointed out. "It would just roll down to the bottom."

"Exactly. That would make it more fun! Uphill football, I've just invented it. I might be famous!"

Sophie shook her head. "I don't think all the people taking photos would be very impressed either. There are loads of them. They'd tell you off."

"Huh." But Dan looked round at all the visitors, and realized Sophie was right. No one looked as if they wanted to play football. And there was an old lady sitting on the bench over there with a really pointy umbrella, the kind with a parrot's head handle. She looked like she'd happily use the pointy end to stab footballs, and even the parrot seemed to be giving him a fierce glare.

"Race you up and down the balustrades then!" He grabbed her hand and hurried her down the two flights of stairs to the path.

Sophie squirmed. The balustrades were the stone slopes at the sides of the steps. They were wide and flat, and Dan loved to run up and down them. He'd discovered the game the first time they came to visit the church, just after they'd moved to Paris, and since *Sacré Coeur* was on their way home from school, he'd been practising. But the game made Sophie feel sick, especially when it had been raining and the stone was all slick and slippery. She was sure that he would fall off.

"Come on, Sophie!" Dan hopped up to the stonework. "You get up on the other side. Bet I can beat you back to the top!"

Sophie stood on the bottom step, looking anxiously at the flat white slope. She didn't want to run up it — but if she refused, Dan would keep on and on teasing her.

"Baby!" her brother called scornfully, and Sophie scowled. She was only a year younger than Dan! She was not a baby! Carefully, the tip of her tongue sticking out between her teeth, she stepped on to the balustrade. It wasn't really so very high, after all... And Dan looked so surprised that she'd done it! Sophie grinned at him.

"Go!" Dan yelled, dashing away up the slope. Sophie gasped, and raced after him,

wishing she had trainers on, and not her
best shoes with the glittery bows.

She slithered a little, and gasped and
reached out her hands to balance,
wishing there was something to hold on
to – a tree maybe. But there was only
the perfect short green grass, and every

so often those funny little cone-shaped bushes that almost looked like upside-down ice creams.

Halfway to the top, Dan let out a yell as he spotted one of his friends from school on the other side of the hill. He hopped down and raced across the grass to see Benjamin, leaving Sophie glaring after him. He'd just abandoned their race, after she'd been brave enough to climb the balustrade at last. How could he? She folded her arms and tapped her foot crossly on the stone. Brothers! They were so rude!

If only she had a friend to play with, too. It wasn't fair. Sophie watched Dan and Benjamin chasing each other across the grass, and sighed sadly. Somehow, she just hadn't found anybody she liked that much at school yet. Even though Mum had spoken French to them ever since they were little, Sophie still felt as though she wasn't doing it quite right. The teachers told her she was doing ever so well, but the girls in her class looked at her funny whenever she opened her mouth. And then they just ran off. After some days at school, Sophie wondered if she might forget how to talk at all. It was nothing like back home. Mum had suggested sending emails to her friends from their school in London, and Sophie had, but it wasn't the same at all. All the fun things that Elizabeth and Zara told her in their replies only made Sophie feel more left out.

The only girls who'd really spoken to her were Chloe and Adrienne, and that was because their teacher had asked them to look after the new girl. Sophie had decided halfway through the first morning that she'd much rather be unlooked-after. Chloe didn't do anything except twitch her nose and giggle, which was boring, though bearable, but Sophie thought

Adrienne was possibly the nastiest pers[on]
she had ever met. Because her voice was
so sweet and soft, the things she
said sounded perfectly nice at
first. It was only when Sophie
thought back that she realized
how horrible they actually were.

"So, why *did* you move here?"
Adrienne had a way of looking at Sophie
with her head on one side that made
Sophie feel like she was some ugly sort
of beetle.

"Your French is quite good. For an
English person, I mean..."

"I suppose that's an *English* skirt. It's
very ... interesting."

Sophie gave a little shiver, even though the sun was warm on her bare shoulders. It was a hot September afternoon, but Adrienne's pretty voice was like cold water trickling down her spine, even when she was only remembering it.

She sighed again, and then shuddered as Dan and Benjamin started a race, rolling down the grassy slope.

And then she fell off.

Afterwards, Sophie wasn't quite sure how she did it. She hadn't even been moving. But her feet seemed to slip suddenly from underneath her, and then her arms were flapping uselessly at the air. There was a thump, and she was flat on the grass on her tummy, next to one of those strange little cone-shaped bushes.

Sophie lay there, gasping and trying not to cry. She wanted Dan to come and pick her up – but at the same time she didn't want him knowing she'd been silly enough to fall.

"Are you all right?"

It wasn't Dan. The mystery voice was speaking in French, and Dan would have spoken to her in English. It just didn't sound like Dan, anyway. Sophie hoped it wasn't the old lady with the parrot umbrella. She would probably say it was all Sophie's own fault, and insist on taking her back to Mum and Dad and

Auntie Lou and the endless photographs.

But surely even a very little old lady wouldn't have such a high, squeaky voice?

Sophie turned her head slightly, and squeaked herself.

Staring at her worriedly was a tiny furry face, ginger-and-white, with neat little ears, and shining eyes.

"Are you hurt?" the squeaky voice said again, and this time there was no doubt about it. It was definitely this small furry person who was talking to her.

"No, I'm not. Thank you for asking,"

Sophie whispered, trying to sit up.

"Oh, good. Yes, that's right. Much better." The guinea pig — for now that she was the right way up, Sophie could see that's what the furry little person was — nodded approvingly. "You didn't hit your head?"

"I don't think so," Sophie murmured, shaking it gently. Though if she had bumped her head, it would explain why she was talking to a guinea pig. And, more importantly, how the guinea pig seemed to be talking back.

"Are you imaginary?" she asked, wondering if she had actually hit her head *very hard*.

"Certainly not!" The guinea pig's voice became even squeakier. Sophie was surprised it could manage it. "Whatever gave you that idea?" it asked indignantly.

"Well. You're talking. And ... and you've got a pink ballet skirt on."

The guinea pig looked down at her middle — now she'd noticed the skirt, Sophie was guessing that the guinea pig was probably a girl. Then she flounced the skirt with her little pink paws and did a twirl, gazing at her plump middle with a great deal of satisfaction. "I know. I found it yesterday. Do you like it? I think it suits me very well. But I suppose you haven't seen that many guinea pigs wearing clothes

before. I can see why you'd be surprised."

"Actually, my friend Elizabeth from home is always trying to dress up her hamster," Sophie admitted. "But he bites her, every time. It was really the talking that seemed so unusual."

"Oh..." The guinea pig looked faintly worried, and her tiny round ears twitched. "It's just possible that I shouldn't have spoken to you. It *is* meant to be a secret, actually. But I was frightened that you were hurt. You were lying so still. I'm sure the others will understand." She smoothed the pink net of her skirt with anxious little pats of her paws.

"I promise I won't tell anybody," Sophie said quickly. "It was very nice of you to be worried about me." Then she frowned. "But if you're supposed to be a secret, should you be standing there like that? Everyone can see you."

The guinea pig let out a panicked

breath of a squeak. "Mercy me! I
haven't even got my hat on! Do excuse
me a moment." She whisked round,
and disappeared under the little cone-
shaped bush in a blur of ginger fur and
shocking-pink net.

A minute later she was back, with a
neat circle of grass attached to the top
of her head. It was held on with a
green ribbon, tied in a large bow under
her chin.

"We'll be all right now," the guinea
pig told Sophie. "Thank you for noticing,
I can't think how I came to be so
careless. I'll forget my own name next.
It's Josephine," she added. "I didn't tell

you, did I?" She
bobbed Sophie
a little curtsey,
holding out the
ballet skirt with
her paws.

Sophie looked
around nervously. She
wasn't sure that the grassy hat was
actually enough of a disguise. The
guinea pig still looked very much like
a guinea pig, except that now she had
long green tufty hair. There were people
climbing the stone steps past them all the
time. She wondered if she should offer to
let the guinea pig hide under the edge of

her skirt. "It's very nice to meet you. I'm Sophie. But. . ."

"I promise. . ." A little pink paw was resting on Sophie's lap. "No one will see. We've been here for so many years, you know. And no one ever does notice us. After all, it's such a silly story! A family of guinea pigs living underneath the beautiful church of *Sacré Coeur*? No one would ever believe it!"

"But I can see you," Sophie pointed out.

"Ah, if you're clever enough to see what I really am, you're clever enough to know that you must never, ever tell." Josephine's sparkling black eyes gazed hopefully into Sophie's blue ones, and Sophie nodded.

"Of course I won't. Unless ... I'm not very good at keeping secrets from Dan. He's my brother. I will if I have to, though."

"Hmmm. Well. A brother might be all right," Josephine said cautiously. "I shall have to see him first, to make sure."

Sophie nodded. "Did you really say that there were more of you?"

"Oh, yes. Our tunnels stretch all the way under the hill," Josephine explained, sitting down comfortably next to Sophie, and spreading out her pink skirt. "And it's a good thing too. It's very hard work. We couldn't possibly manage with any fewer of us." She waved a paw proudly across the soft green turf. "Look at it. Beautifully neat and tidy."

Sophie opened her mouth and then shut it again, looking at the grass. "You mean, that's what you do?" she asked at last. "You cut the grass?"

"Certainly we do! You don't think they could ever get a lawnmower up such a steep slope, do you? Why, it would just fall straight off!" The little guinea pig shuddered at the thought, and then peered down the hill. "It would be just like those two silly boys," she added, waving a paw at Dan and Benjamin, who were rolling over and over in a tangle of arms and legs. "The city council did send someone to cut it once, or so my great-great-great grandfather said. The poor man broke a leg, and said never again. But somehow, strangely enough, the grass here just never seems to get any longer." She winked at Sophie. "Isn't that lucky? Of course, now that there are so many visitors, we have to tidy up as well. We don't mind, though. Sometimes we find the nicest things." She looked at her pink tutu, and then up at Sophie, who said hurriedly, "Oh, yes. That ballet skirt really does suit you."

"Yummy things to eat too," Josephine
said, resting a paw on her plump ginger
stomach. "Lavender macarons are my
favourite, from the shop across the road.
Such a pretty colour. Unfortunately,
people just don't drop those very often."

"I suppose not... But I thought
that guinea pigs only ate grass and seeds
and things."

"That would be rather boring,
wouldn't it? And anyway, lavender
macarons taste like flowers," Josephine
said firmly. "Delicious. Of course, I
couldn't manage a whole one." She
looked thoughtful. "Although I could

try." Then she twisted round and gasped. "Someone's coming!"

Sophie looked round too, and saw Dan, running up the balustrade towards them, arms stretched sideways to balance. "That's my brother," she started to explain, but Josephine was gone. Completely gone, disappeared, and so quickly that it was as if she had never been there at all.

Sophie sat with her mouth open, her eyes suddenly stinging with tears.

She *had* imagined it! She blinked and sniffed, and told herself that she should have known. "You are a baby," she whispered sadly to herself. "It's no wonder no one at that school likes you." She wrapped her arms around her middle, feeling chilly. It was as if the warmth had suddenly gone out of the afternoon.

After all, who would ever believe that there was a family of guinea pigs, living under the hill? It was such a silly story...

But then, that was exactly what Josephine had said. She'd stared straight at Sophie, with sparkling black eyes, and said that only the very cleverest people would ever see what she really was.

"Could I really have made it up?" Sophie whispered to herself, looking at the beautifully short, tidy grass. It did look *exactly* as though it was nibbled away to neatness every night by a family of guinea pigs...